When I sat down at the table for breakfast, the doll was at my place. Mama had made hair out of dark brown yarn and she'd embroidered eyes, a nose, and a mouth on the face. She had covered the yarn hair with a yellow kerchief embroidered with red flowers.

"She's gorgeous, Mama," I managed to murmur. "But she doesn't look like the Pilgrim woman in the picture."

"No?" Mama said.

"She looks like you in that photograph you have that was taken when you were a girl."

"Of course," Mama said. "I did that on purpose. What's a Pilgrim, *shaynkeit*? A Pilgrim is someone who came here from the other side to find freedom. That's me, Molly. I'm a Pilgrim!"

Molly's Pilgrim

by Barbara Cohen
Illustrated by Michael J. Deraney

A BANTAM SKYLARK BOOK
NEW YORK • TORONTO • LONDON • SYDNEY • AUCKLAND

RL 3, 005–008

MOLLY'S PILGRIM

A Bantam Skylark Book / published by arrangement with
William Morrow and Company, Inc.

PRINTING HISTORY
William Morrow edition published 1983
Bantam edition / November 1990

Skylark Books is a registered trademark of Bantam Books, a
division of Bantam Doubleday Dell Publishing Group, Inc.
Registered in U.S. Patent and Trademark Office and elsewhere.

ISBN 0-553-15833-3

Published simultaneously in the United States and Canada

Bantam Books are published by Bantam Books, a division of Bantam Doubleday Dell Publishing Group, Inc. Its trademark,
consisting of the words "Bantam Books" and the portrayal of a
rooster, is Registered in U.S. Patent and Trademark Office and in
other countries. Marca Registrada. Bantam Books, 666 Fifth Ave-
nue, New York, New York 10103.

PRINTED IN THE UNITED STATES OF AMERICA

CWO   0 9

*In honor of
all the family stories
that I heard during my childhood,
and in memory of the tellers,
heroes, and villains of those tales—
my grandfather, Harry Marshall,
and my great aunt, Molly Marshall Hyman,
to say nothing of all the others—
Uncle Jake, Uncle Ike, Uncle Abe, Uncle Henry,
and even Aunt Fanny.*

BC

To my sister, Pat
MJD

I didn't like the school in Winter
Hill. In Winter Hill they laughed
at me.

Elizabeth laughed most of all. I never raised my hand to answer a question, but when Miss Stickley called on me, I had to say something. My English wasn't perfect yet, so Elizabeth always giggled at whatever I said. Miss Stickley would stare at her, and then she'd shut up. But later, in the schoolyard, she'd say, "You talk funny, Molly. You look funny, Molly." And then she'd sing a song.

Jol-ly Mol-ly,
Your eyes are awf'ly small.
Jol-ly Mol-ly,
Your nose is awf'ly tall.

Hilda and Kitty would sing the
song, too, and sometimes even
Fay and Emma. They all
admired Elizabeth. She brought
peppermint sticks to school and
handed them out to all her
friends at recess.

One day Elizabeth and Hilda
followed me halfway home,
singing that terrible song.

Jol-ly Mol-ly,
Your eyes are awf'ly small.
Jol-ly Mol-ly,
Your nose is awf'ly tall.

I started to run. When I got to our apartment, I burst into tears. It was all right. I could cry in front of my mother.

She put her arms around me. I leaned my head against her chest. She felt like a big, soft cushion. *"Shaynkeit,* what's the matter?" she asked. My mother didn't speak much English. She talked to me in Yiddish.

"Mama, let's go back to New York City," I said. "In this third grade, there aren't any other Jewish children. I don't talk like the other girls. They make fun of me. I hate going to school."

"*Oi, Malkeleh,*" Mama said, "we can't go back to New York City. In New York, Papa had to work in a factory. We had to live in a poor tenement house. Here in Winter Hill, Papa has a good job in Mr. Brodsky's store downstairs, and Mr. Brodsky even lets us live in this nice apartment."

"Well, then, let's go back to Goraduk," I suggested. "We only came to this country last winter. I bet we could still get our old house back."

"If the Cossacks haven't burned it down," Mama snapped. "They burned the synagogue. One day, who knows, they would have burned us. May they grow like onions, with their heads in the ground."

I had known all along we couldn't go back to Russia.

"In Goraduk, Jewish girls don't get to go to school at all," Mama went on. "They have to grow up ignorant, like donkeys. I'll go to your school, I'll talk to the teacher. She'll make those *paskudnyaks* stop teasing you."

"No, Mama, no!" I interrupted quickly. "You don't have to do that." I didn't want Miss Stickley or Elizabeth to see Mama. She didn't talk like the other mothers; she hardly talked English at all.

She didn't look like them, either. "It'll be all right," I said. "I'll talk to Miss Stickley myself."

But of course I didn't. I dragged myself back to that school day after day. Nothing changed, but I didn't say another word about it to Mama.

Then one day in November, during Reading, Miss Stickley said, "Open your books to page one hundred and thirty-two." It was a new story. I liked it when we started a new story.

"You may begin, Molly," Miss Stickley said.

I looked at the title. "The First . . . The First Th . . . Th . . . Th . . ." I shook my head. "Miss Stickley," I said, "I don't know that word."

"It's a hard word, Molly," Miss Stickley said, "especially if you haven't seen it before. Who can tell Molly what that word is?"

Several hands shot up. Miss Stickley called on Elizabeth. "Thanksgiving," she announced, tossing her long black corkscrew curls. "I thought everyone knew that."

"Thanksgiving?" I repeated. "Thanksgiving? What's Thanksgiving?"

Elizabeth snorted. "You don't even know about Thanksgiving? I guess you people don't celebrate American holidays."

Miss Stickley ignored Elizabeth. "The story will explain the word, Molly," she said to me. "Go ahead, start reading."

I read three sentences. I didn't stumble over any more words. Then Miss Stickley told Arthur to read. We took turns. It was a good story. It was about the Pilgrims and how they started the holiday of Thanksgiving. I had never heard of Pilgrims before.

"Now, children," Miss Stickley said when the reading lesson was over, "I'm tired of decorating the room with paper turkeys and paper pumpkins every Thanksgiving. I thought it would be fun to do something different this year." She pointed to the sand table at the back of the room. It had stood empty since September. "We'll make a model of the Pilgrim village at Plymouth, Massachusetts, celebrating the first Thanksgiving." She sounded excited. "We'll make the houses and the church here in school.

But I want you to make the people at home. You can make dolls out of clothespins. The boys can make Indians and the girls can make Pilgrims." Her eyes moved from one face to another. "If you sit in row one, two, or three, make a woman. If you sit in row four, five, or six, make a man."

I sat in row two. I had to make a Pilgrim woman.

"Bring your dolls tomorrow," Miss Stickley said. "Then I'll show you how to make houses out of cardboard."

When I got home, Mama said to me, just like always, "*Nu, shaynkeit*, do you have any homework?"

"I need a clothespin," I said.

"A clothespin? What kind of homework is a clothespin?"

"I have to make a doll out of it. A Pilgrim doll."

Mama frowned. "*Nu, Malkeleh*, what's a Pilgrim?"

I searched for the words to explain "Pilgrim" to Mama. "Pilgrims came to this country from the other side," I said.

"Like us," Mama said.

That was true. "They came for religious freedom," I added. "They came so they could worship God as they pleased."

Mama's eyes lit up. She seemed to understand. "Do you have any other homework?" she asked.

"Yes," I said. "I have ten arithmetic problems. They're hard."

"Do them," she said, "and then go out to play. I'll make the doll for you. I'll make it tonight. It'll be ready for you in the morning."

"Just make sure it's a girl doll," I said.

"Naturally," Mama replied. "Who ever heard of a boy doll?"

I didn't bother to explain.

The next morning, when I sat down at the table for breakfast, the doll was at my place. Maybe she had started out as a clothespin, but you'd never have known it to look at her. Mama had covered the clothespin with cloth and stuffing. She had made hair out of dark brown yarn and she'd embroidered eyes, a nose, and a mouth on the face. She had dressed the doll in a long, full red skirt, tiny black felt boots, and a bright yellow high-necked blouse. She had covered the yarn hair with a

yellow kerchief embroidered
with red flowers.

"She's gorgeous, Mama," I
managed to murmur.

Mama smiled, satisfied.

"But Mama," I added slowly,
"she doesn't look like the Pilgrim
woman in the picture in my
reading book."

"No?" Mama said.

"She looks like you in that
photograph you have that was
taken when you were a girl."

Mama's smile turned into a laugh. "Of course. I did that on purpose."

"You did, Mama? Why?"

"What's a Pilgrim, *shaynkeit*?" Mama asked. "A Pilgrim is someone who came here from the other side to find freedom. That's me, Molly. I'm a Pilgrim!"

I was sure there was
something wrong with what
Mama was saying. She was not
the kind of Pilgrim Miss Stickley
or the reading book had been
talking about. But it was too late
to make another doll now. All I
could do was take the only one I
had to school with me.

Most of the dolls were out on
the desks. I had carried mine in
a little paper bag. I put it inside
my desk without even taking it
out of the bag.

The bell hadn't rung yet.
Elizabeth and Hilda were
walking up and down the aisles,
pointing to the dolls and
whispering. When they came to

my desk, Elizabeth said in a low voice, "Miss Stickley's going to be mad at you, jolly Molly. She doesn't like people who don't do their homework."

"I did it," I muttered.

"Well, then, let's see it."

I shook my head.

"You didn't do it," Elizabeth taunted. "You didn't, you didn't."

I opened the desk and took out the paper bag. I closed the desk and set the bag on top. Slowly, I pulled out the doll.

"Oh, my goodness," Elizabeth
sighed. "How can anyone be as
dumb as you, jolly Molly? That's

not a Pilgrim. Miss Stickley is going to be really mad at you. Miss Stickley's going to get you this time."

My face felt hot as fire. I looked down at my desktop.

The bell rang. Elizabeth and Hilda rushed to their seats. I shoved the doll back into my desk.

After morning exercises, Miss Stickley began to walk around the room, just as Elizabeth had. She looked at each one of the dolls. "Why Michael, what a magnificent headdress. Where did you find so many feathers?

. . . Sally, she's lovely. Such an interesting face. . . . Such beautiful gray silk, Elizabeth. Yours is a very rich Pilgrim."

"I think she's the best so far," Elizabeth said.

"Well, she's very good," Miss Stickley allowed.

Then Miss Stickley came to me. Without looking up, I pulled my doll out of the desk.

I heard Elizabeth laugh out loud. "My goodness, Molly," she cried. "That's not a Pilgrim. That's some Russian or Polish person. What does a person like that have to do with Pilgrims?"

"She's very beautiful," Miss
Stickley said. "Perhaps Molly just
didn't understand."

I looked up at Miss Stickley. "Mama said . . ." I began.

Elizabeth giggled again.

Miss Stickley put her hand on my shoulder. "Tell me what your mama said, Molly."

"This doll is dressed like Mama," I explained slowly. "Mama came to America for religious freedom, too. Mama said she's a Pilgrim."

Elizabeth hooted. She wasn't the only one.

Miss Stickley marched up to the front of the room. She turned and faced the class. "Listen to me, Elizabeth," she said in a loud voice. "Listen to me, all of you. Molly's mother *is* a Pilgrim. She's a modern Pilgrim. She came here, just like the Pilgrims long ago, so she could worship God in her own way, in peace and freedom."

Miss Stickley stared at Elizabeth. "Elizabeth, do you know where the Pilgrims got the idea for Thanksgiving?"

"They just thought it up, Miss Stickley," Elizabeth said.

"No, Elizabeth," Miss Stickley replied. "They read in the Bible about the Jewish harvest holiday of Tabernacles." I knew that holiday. We called it Sukkos.

Miss Stickley was still talking. "The Pilgrims got the idea for Thanksgiving from Jews like Molly and her mama." She marched down the aisle to my desk again. "May I have your doll for a while, Molly?"

"Sure," I said.

"I'm going to put this beautiful doll on my desk," Miss Stickley announced, "where everyone can see it all the time. It will remind us all that Pilgrims are still coming to America." She smiled at me. "I'd like to meet your mama, Molly. Please ask her to come to see me one day after school."

"Your doll is the most beautiful, Molly," Emma said. Emma sat next to me. "Your doll is the most beautiful one of all."

I nodded. "Yes," I said. "I know."

I decided if Miss Stickley

actually invited her, it was all
right for Mama to come to
school. I decided something else,
too. I decided it takes all kinds of
Pilgrims to make a Thanksgiving.

ABOUT THE AUTHOR

Barbara Cohen has written a number of books about Jewish children, including *The Carp in the Bathtub*, which critics have described as a modern classic. Her other books about Jewish children include *The Christmas Revolution* and *The Orphan Game*, both available in Bantam Skylark editions. She received the National Jewish Book Award for children's fiction in 1983, and holds the Sydney Taylor Body-of-Work Award presented by the Association of Jewish Librarians. *Molly's Pilgrim* has been made into a film, and received an Academy Award in 1986. Ms. Cohen lives in Bridgewater, New Jersey.

ABOUT THE ILLUSTRATOR

Michael J. Deraney was born in Grand Forks, North Dakota. He went to college and taught as a special education resource teacher in Minneapolis, Minnesota, before moving to New York City to make art and illustration a full-time career. His work includes the illustrations for *Pot Belly Tales* by Mary Haynes and *Yussel's Prayer* by Barbara Cohen, for which he shares with the author the 1983 National Jewish Book Award.